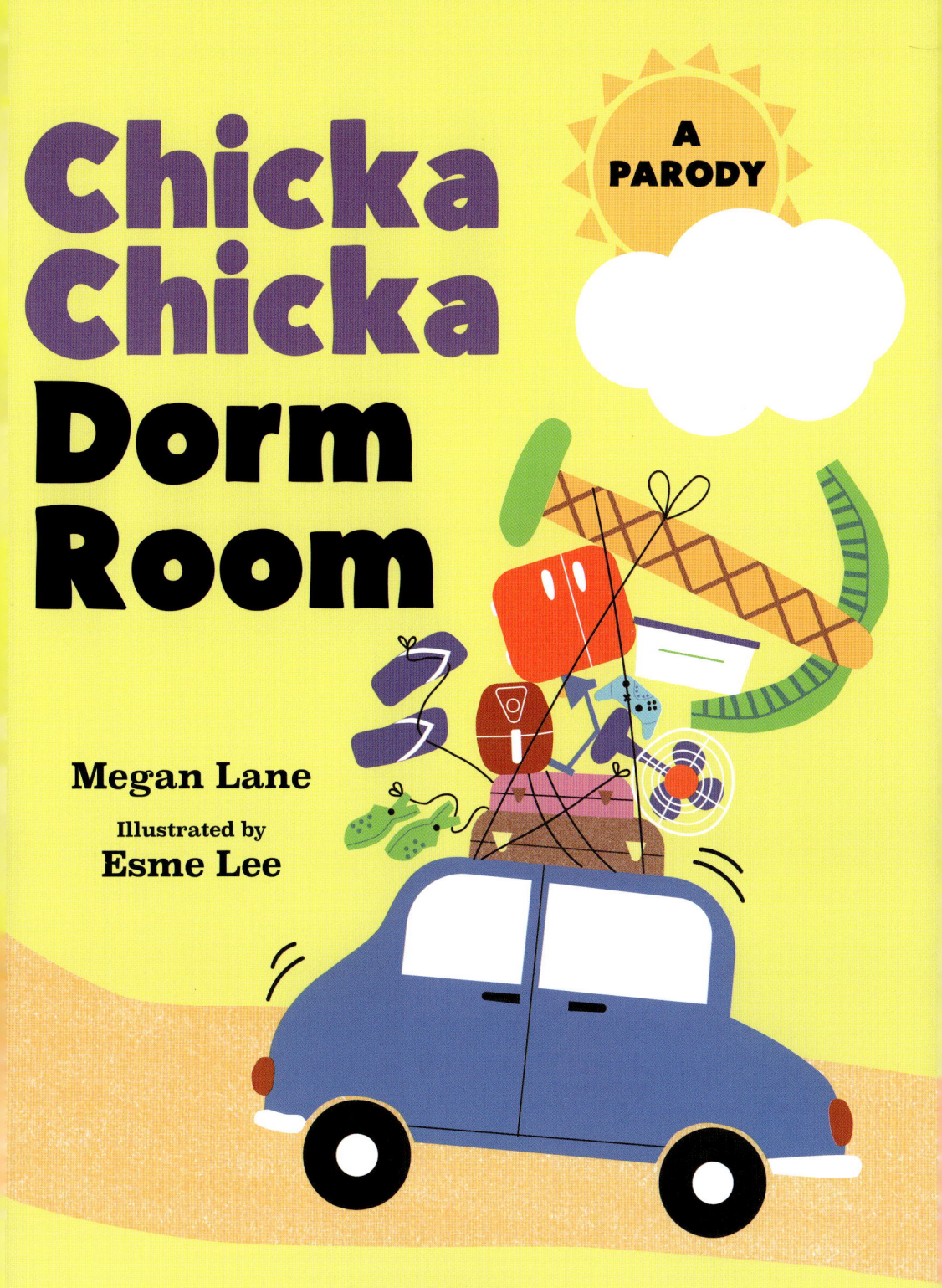

Chicka Chicka Dorm Room

A PARODY

Megan Lane

Illustrated by
Esme Lee

BLUESTONE BOOKS

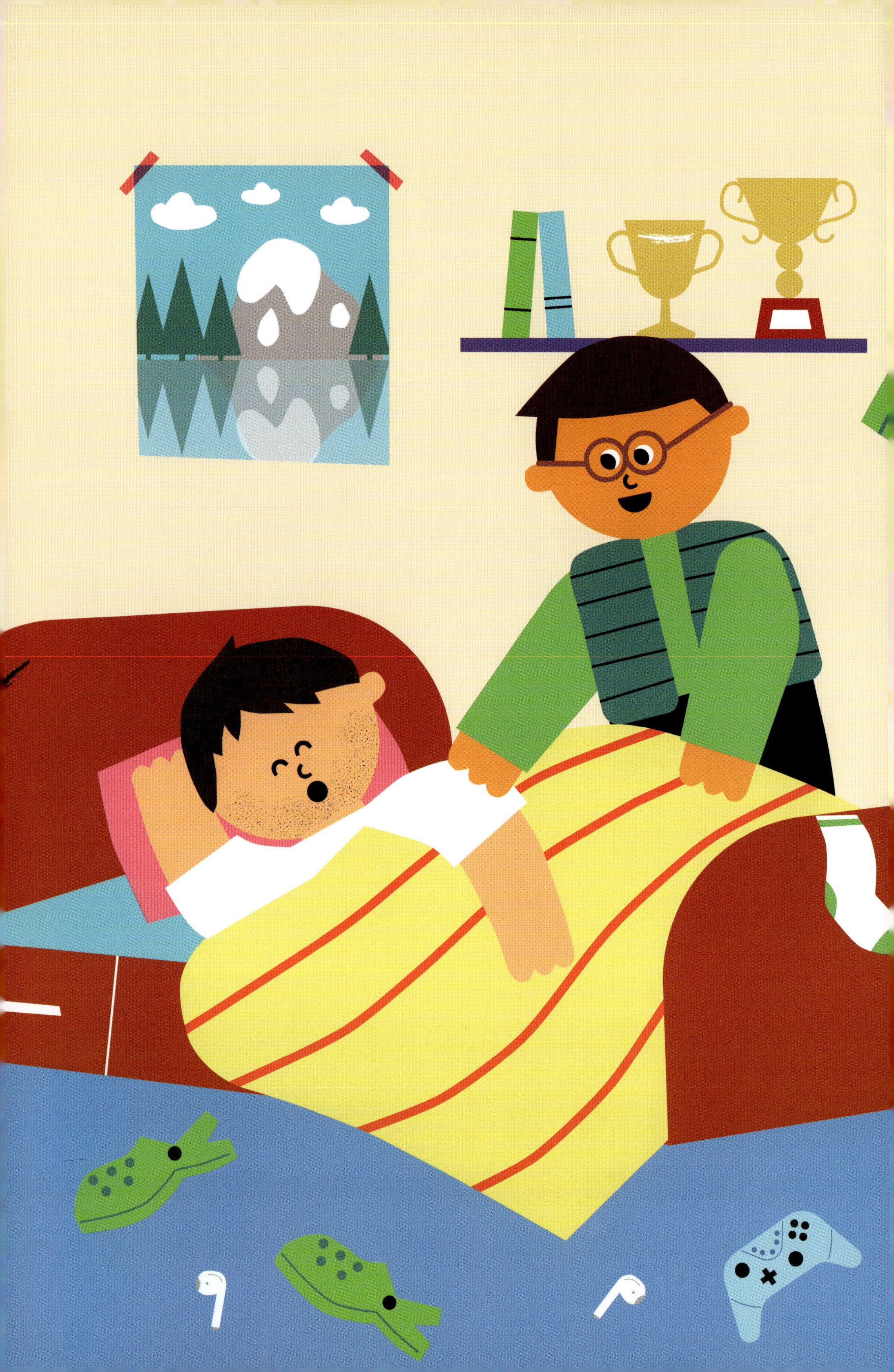

Mom told **Dad**
and Dad told **me**,
"The **dorm rooms** open
at a quarter to **three**."

Skit, skat, little cat,
no time to chill.
Gotta get myself ready,
there's a car to fill!

Chicka chicka **dorm room**,
freshman year begins soon.

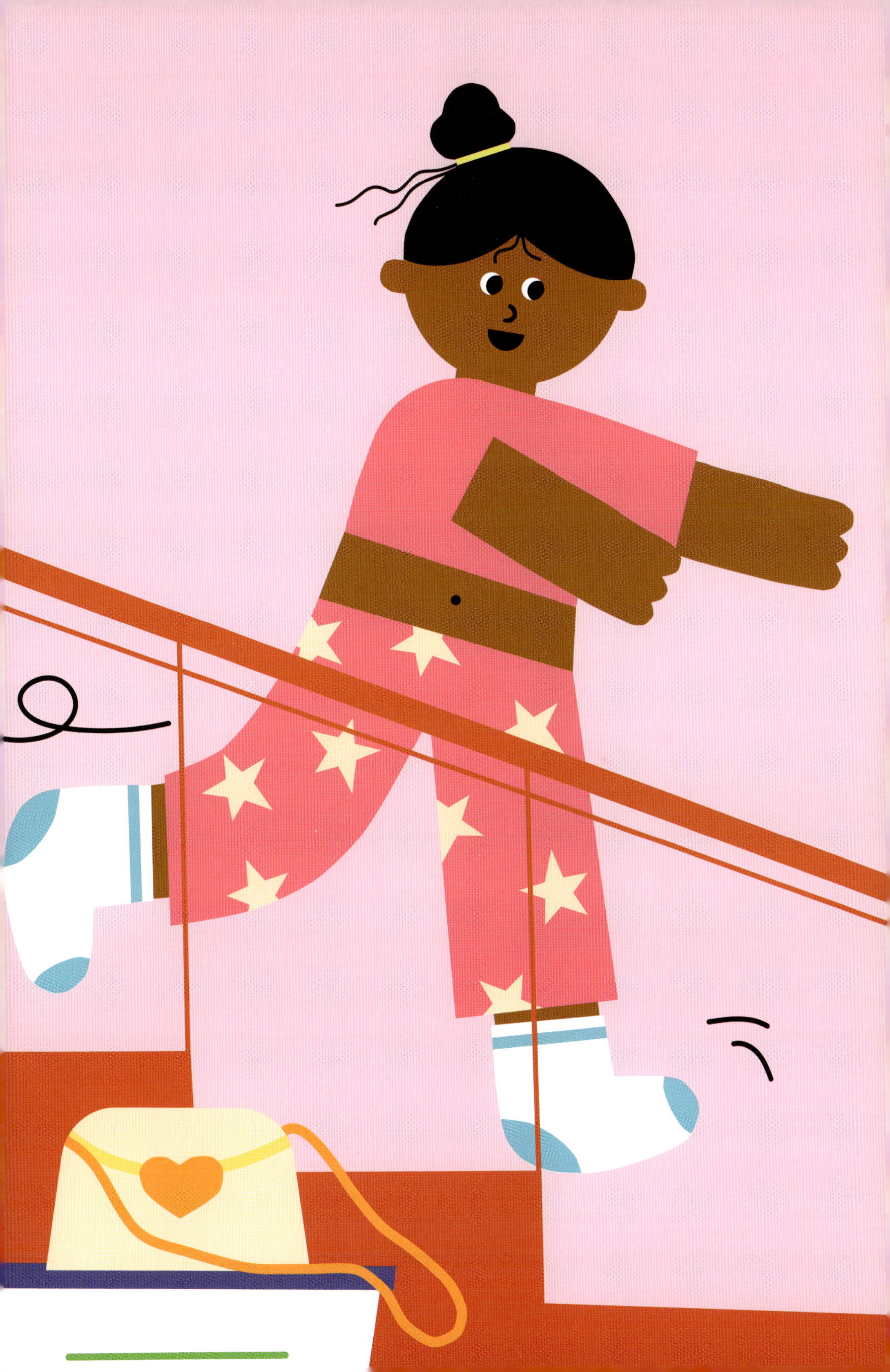

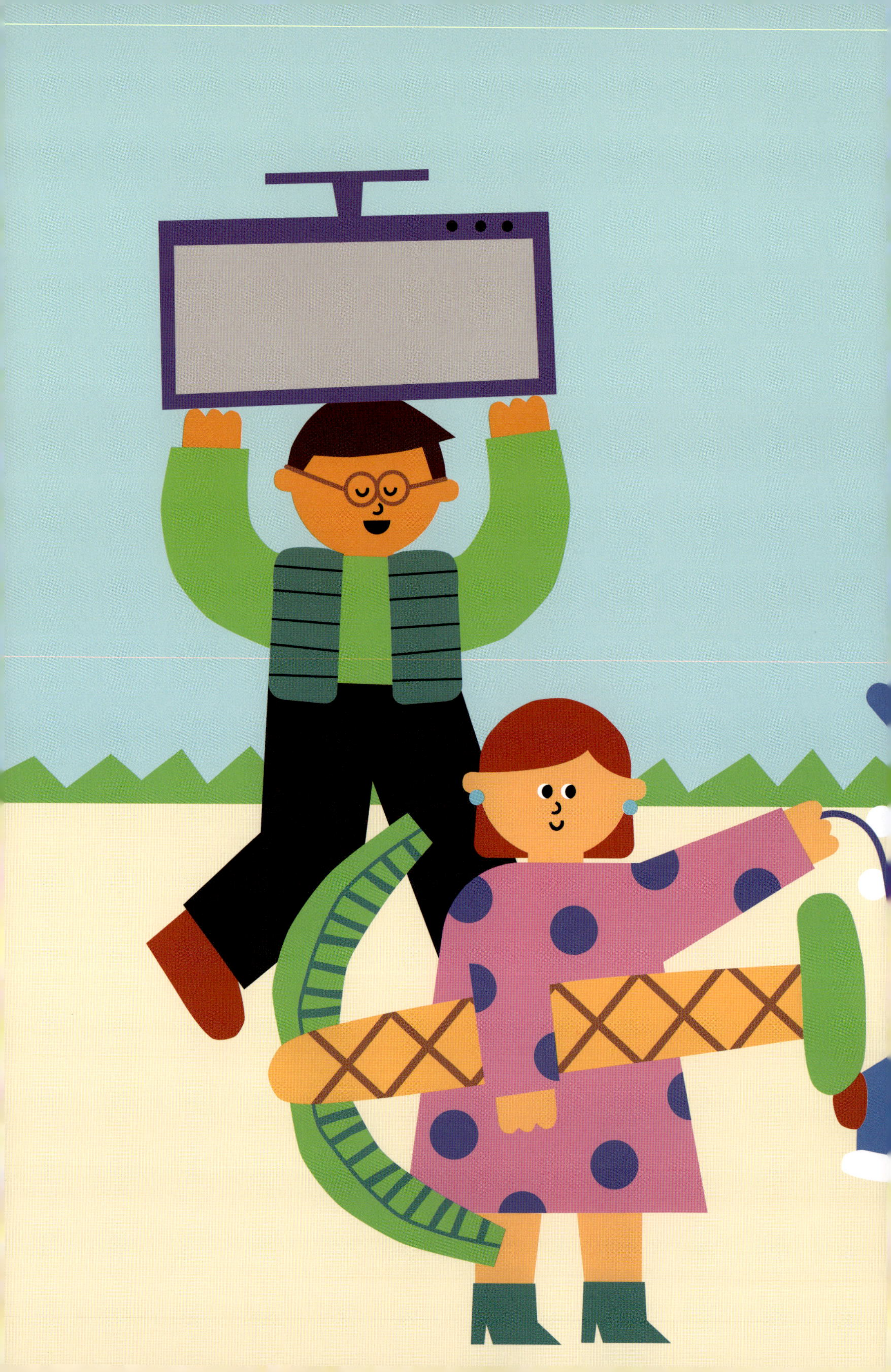

Grab that fan and HDTV.
Here comes big plastic shower caddy.
Bathrobe, string lights, inflatable tree—
"**Are you sure you need it all?**,"
my dad asks me.

Mattress topper, purifier, bed risers, boots.
Body pillow, coffee maker,
mini-fridge—**woot!**

The dog gets loose, runs to and fro,
thinks, "Take me with you when you go."

Pure air

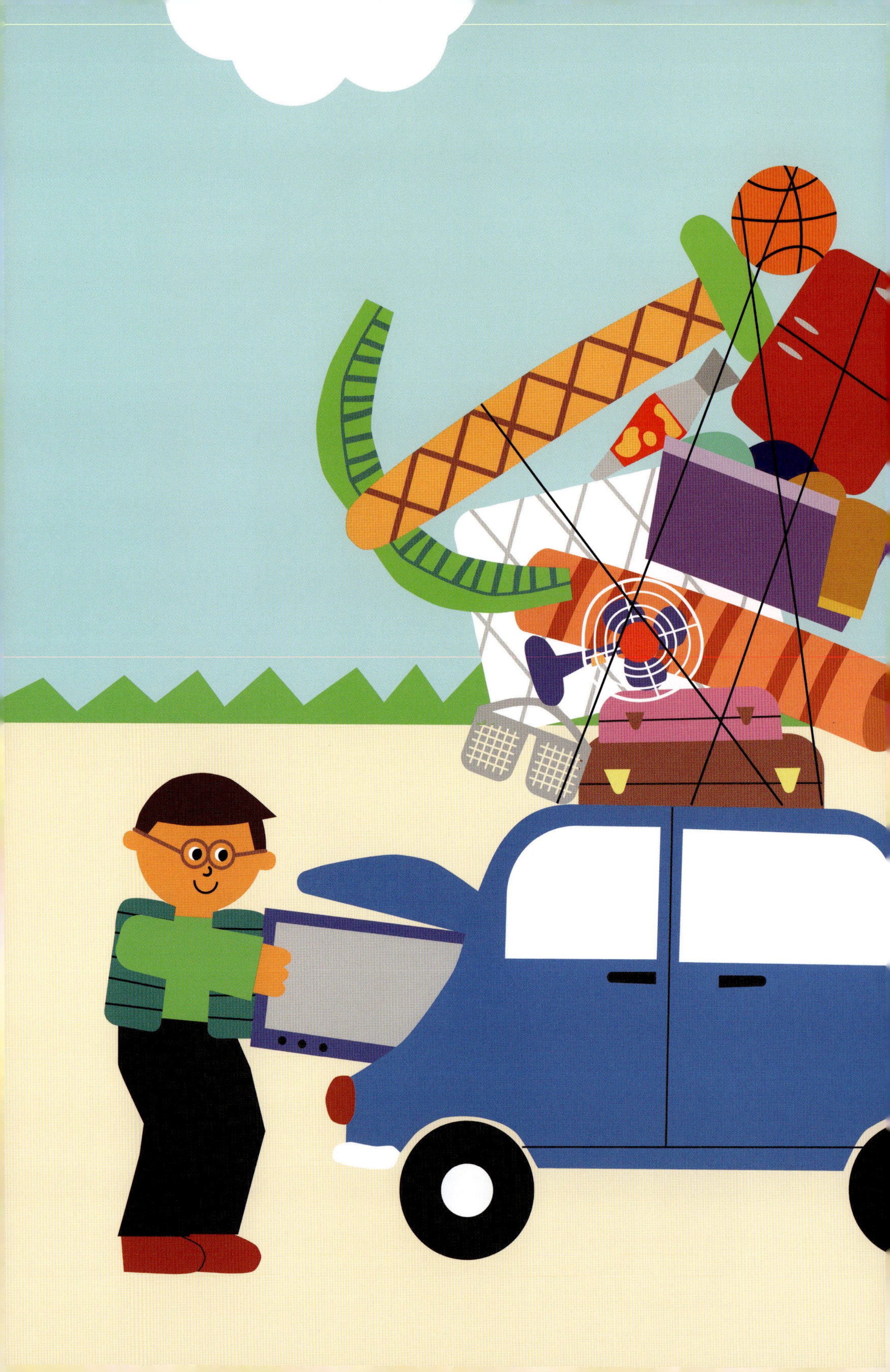

Hand vac, backpack, basketball. **Done!** All from one **mega shopping run.**

My dad is stooped.

I am pooped.

The cords are twisted **alley-oop**.

Chicka Chicka Sweat Swoon, Will there be enough room?

My good friend, Jay, stops by to say, "**Let's hang out** in November when you're **back this way**."

Chicka Chicka Vroom Vroom,
Next stop: **the dorm room!**

My dad pulls up,
I hear a shout.
My roommate's here,
we hug it out.

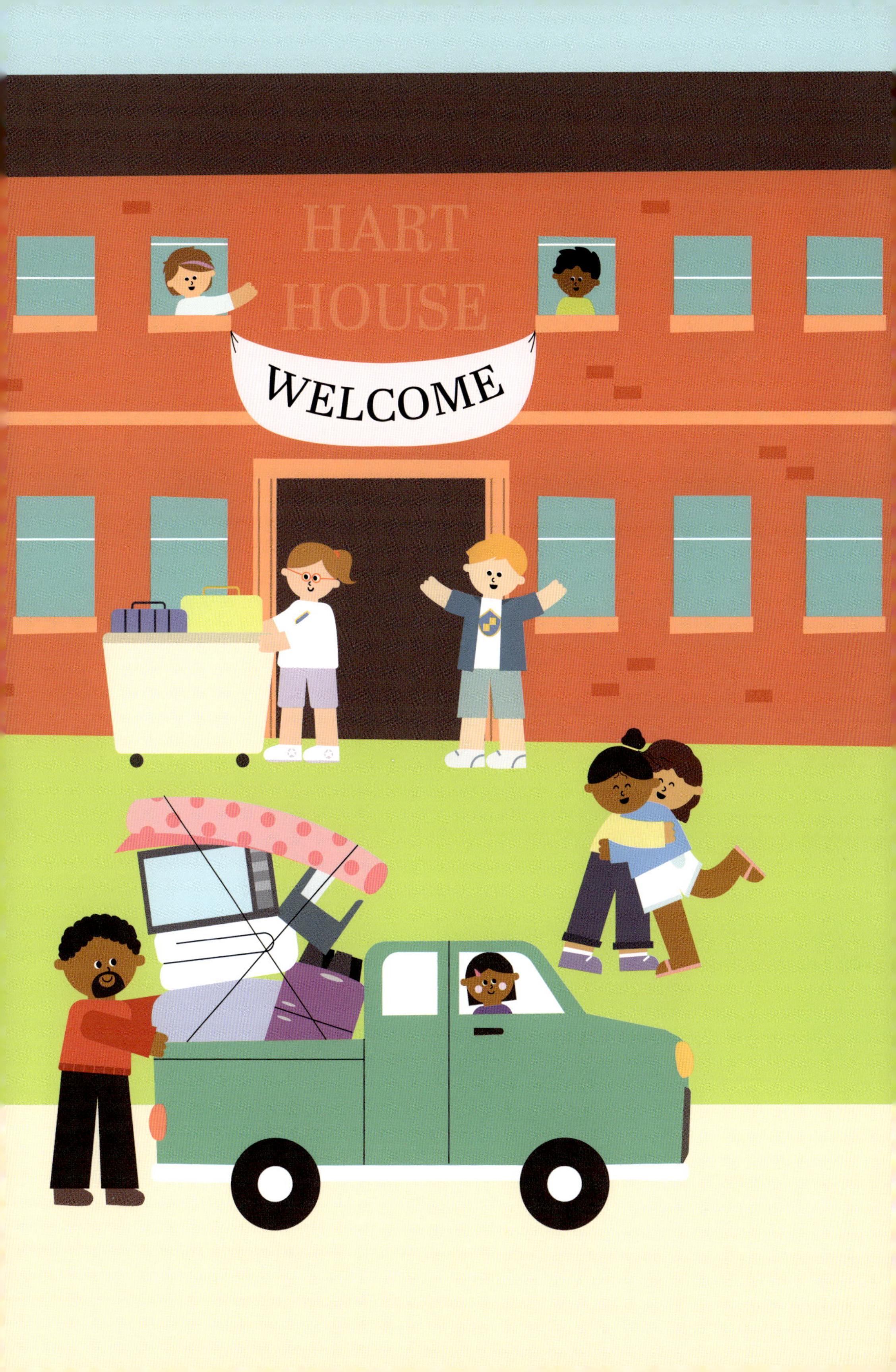
HART HOUSE
WELCOME

Unload. **Unpack.**
Wiggle-jiggle free.
I reach for the
blow-up
coconut tree.

Clatter clunk crash bang.

Tip, teeter, tumble.

It all falls down in a **big old jumble**.

The mamas and the papas

and the college staff

all run over and we share a laugh.

WELCOME

"No worries, man. We're here for you.
Let's get this to Room 202."

Time to set up

all our stuff.

I think we packed more than enough.

Stash, Stack, Style. Box, Bag, Bin.
Our room's so glam—
Let the fun begin!

My mom and dad hug me goodbye.

The sun is setting in the sky.

Time to go.

They've gotta scoot.

(The girl from down the hall looks cute.)

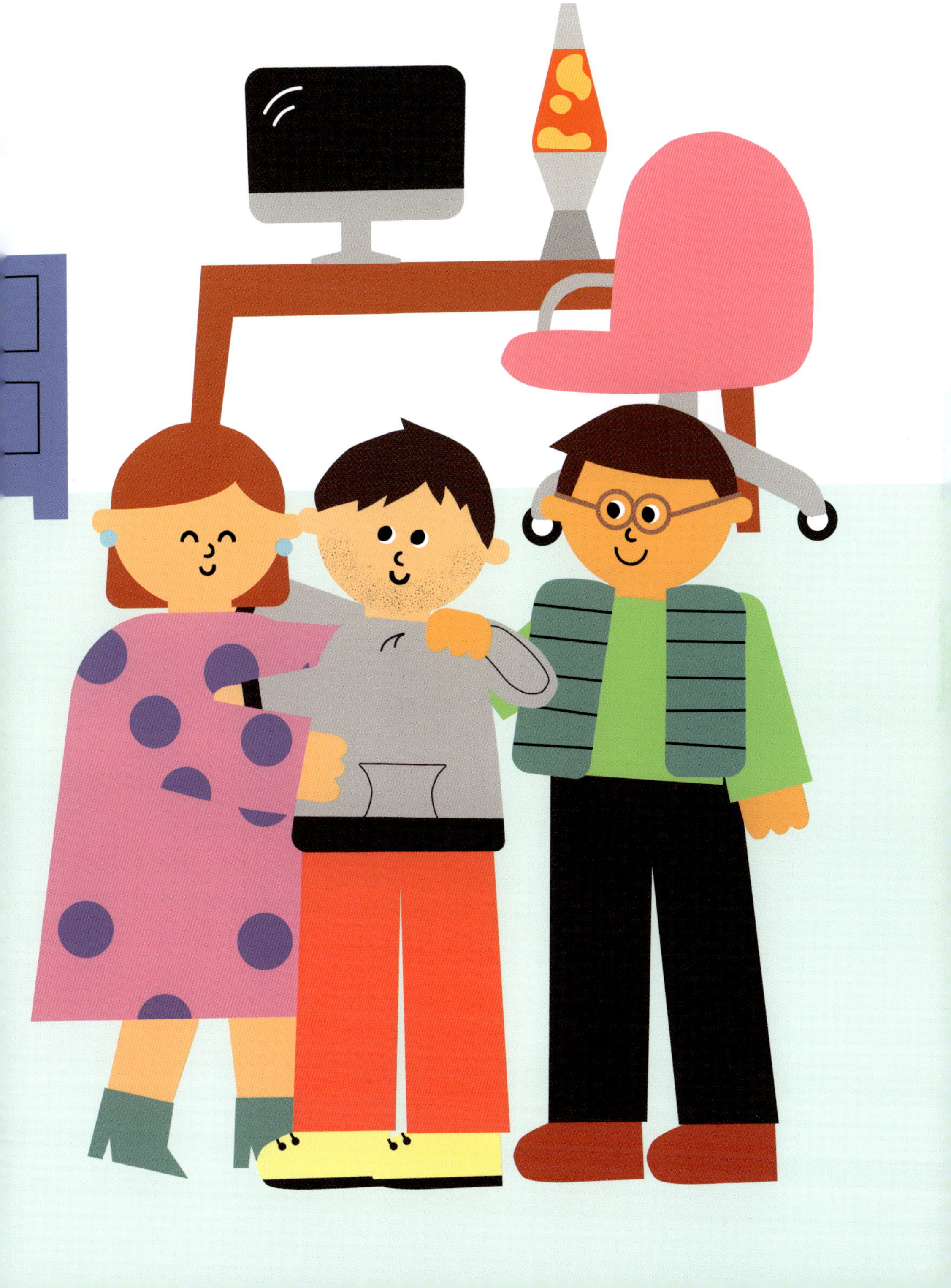

Off to the dining hall.
Flip, flop, flee.

And the sun goes down on the **coconut tree**.

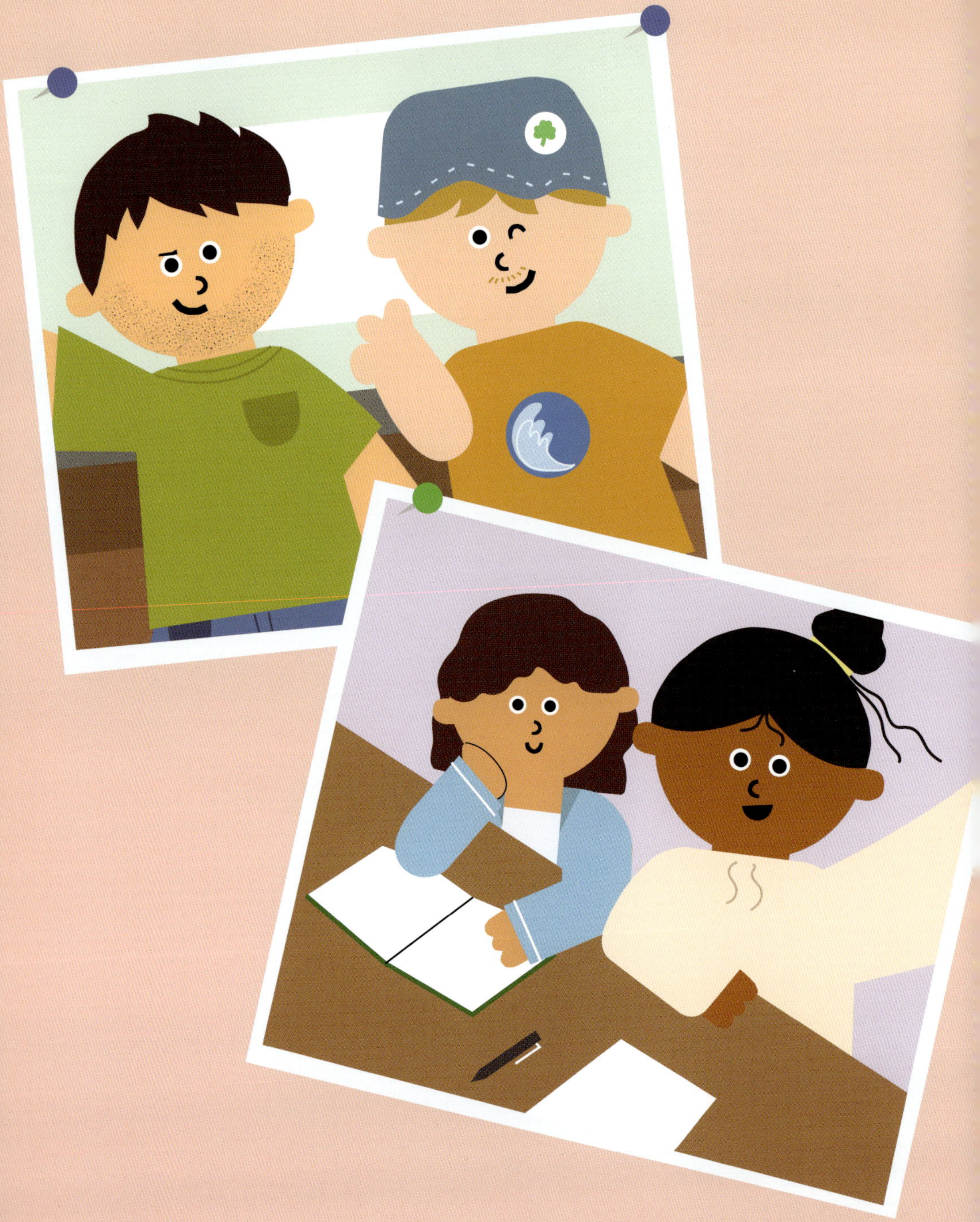

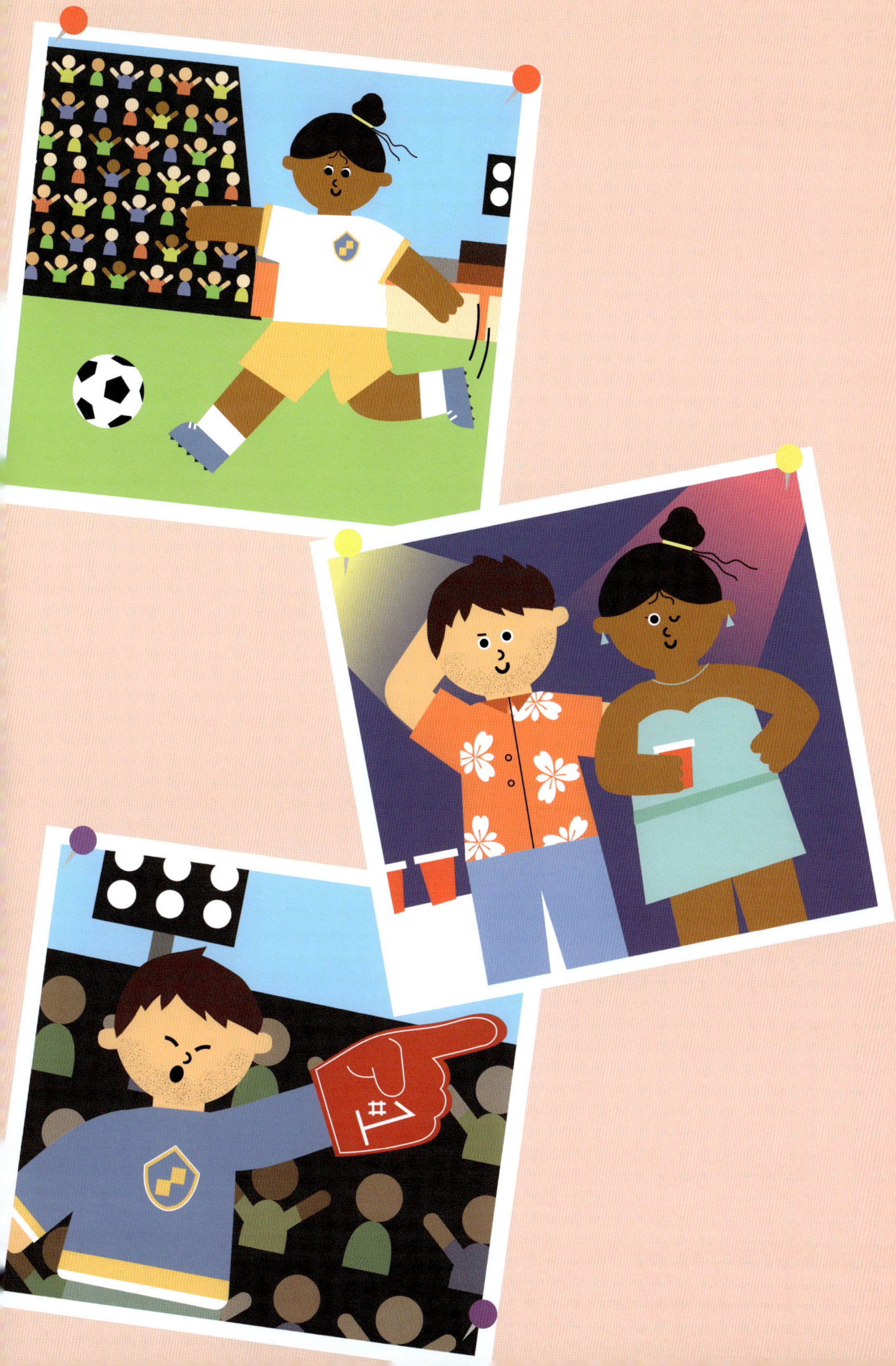
#1

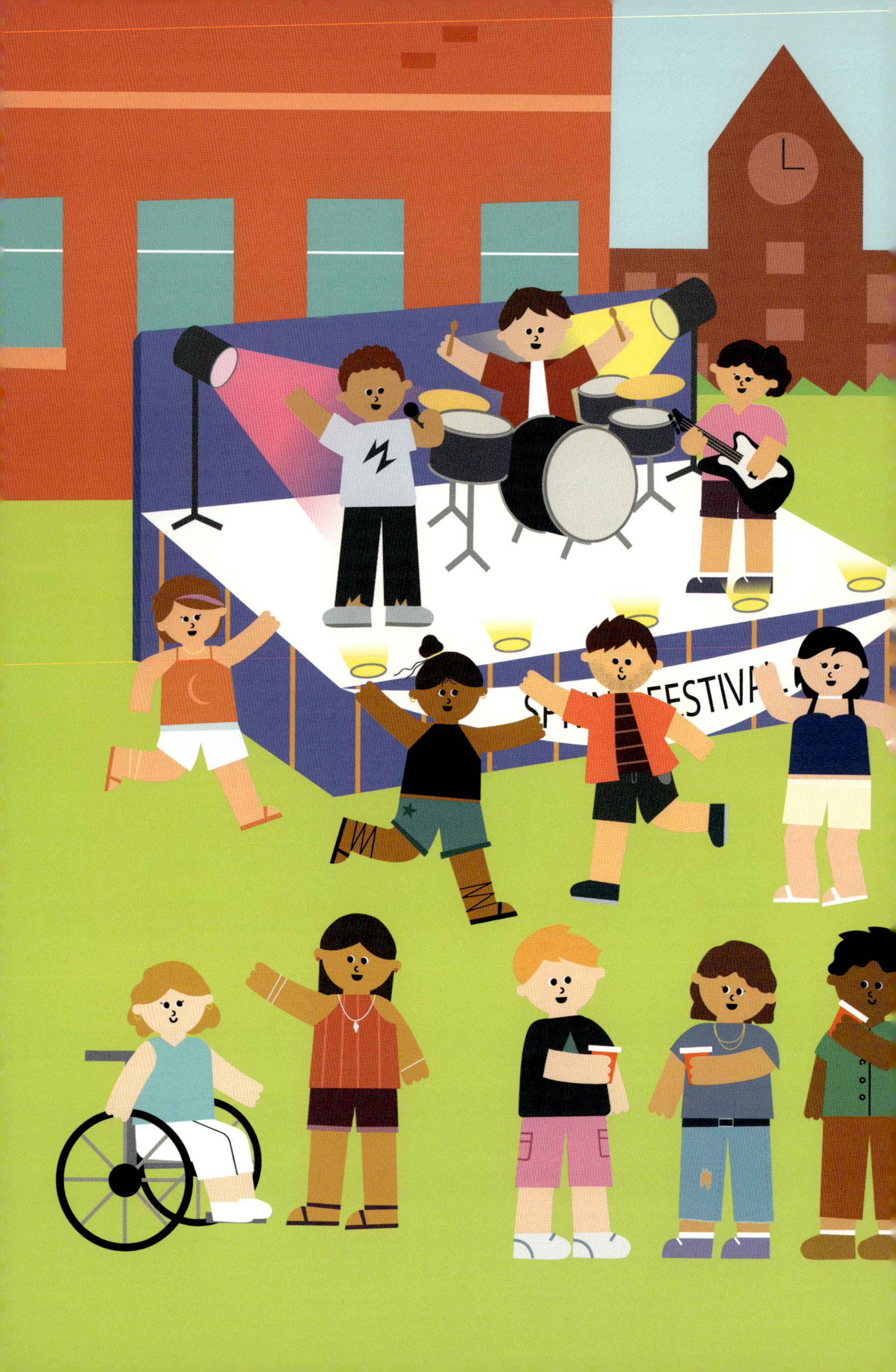

Study hard. Sleep late. I'm in the zone.

The year flew by and I made a home.

Chicka Chicka Dorm Room,

College life in **full bloom.**

Chicka Chicka Dorm Room.
Copyright © 2025 Bluestone Books.
All rights reserved.

Any unauthorized duplication in whole or in part or dissemination
of this edition by any means (including but not limited to
photocopying, electronic devices, digital versions, and the internet)
will be prosecuted to the fullest extent of the law.

Published by Bluestone Books
www.bluestonebooks.co

ISBN: 978-1-965636-01-5 (paper over board)
ISBN: 978-1-965636-10-7 (ebook)

Printed in China

First Edition: 2025

10 9 8 7 6 5 4 3 2 1

. . . .

IMPORTANT NOTE TO READERS:
This book has been written and published for entertainment purposes only.
This book is independently authored and published and no sponsorship or endorsement
of this book by, and no affiliation with *Chicka Chicka Boom Boom* or its creators,
or any trademarked brands or products mentioned within is claimed or suggested.
All trademarks that appear in this book belong to their respective owners and are
used here for informational purposes only. The author and publisher
encourage readers to buy and read *Chicka Chicka Boom Boom*.